MOUSE'S FIRST NIGHT AT
MOONLIGHT SCHOOL

First published 2014 by Nosy Crow Ltd
The Crow's Nest, 10a Lant Street, London SE1 1QR
www.nosycrow.com

ISBN 978 0 85763 118 3 (HB)
ISBN 978 0 85763 119 0 (PB)

A CIP catalogue record for this book is available from the British Library.

Printed in Spain

Papers used by Nosy Crow are made from wood grown in sustainable forests.

1 3 5 7 9 8 6 4 2 (HB)
5 7 9 8 6 4 (PB)

FOR ALL OUR SMALLER SELVES
S.P.

FOR MUM AND DAD, WITH LOVE
A.P.

MOUSE'S FIRST NIGHT AT
MOONLIGHT SCHOOL

SIMON PUTTOCK
Illustrated by ALI PYE

nosy crow

This is Miss Moon's Moonlight School
for all the wee small creatures of the night.

The night bell was about to ring,
and Bat
and Cat
and Owl were all on their way.
But somebody was missing and
that somebody was . . .

...Mouse!
It was Mouse's very first night at Miss Moon's Moonlight School, and Mouse was feeling shy. So she had come in extra early and hidden behind the curtains.

"Has anyone seen our new pupil?"
asked Miss Moon.
"Has anyone seen Mouse?"
Owl put up his wing.

"Yes, Owl?"
asked Miss Moon.

"I have not seen
Mouse," said Owl.

Cat put up her paw.
"I have sadly not seen
Mouse either," she said.

"Bat," asked Miss Moon,
"have YOU seen Mouse?"

"Oh no, Miss Moon," said Bat.
"I have never seen Mouse EVER!"

"How mysterious,"
said Miss Moon.
"Mouse, dear,
are you here?"

Now, Mouse's mother had said to Mouse, "Be sure to be good," so . . .

MAGIC WANDS

EYES OF NEWTS

TOES OF FROGS

NIGHT CREATURES

TALKING TO TREES

MAGICAL SONGS

PLANTS OF MAGIC

FIRST SPELLS

SPELLS v2

HISTORY OF MAGIC

SPELLS v3

. . . "I AM here," said Mouse in a VERY small voice, a voice too small to be properly heard.

"Did somebody
say something?"
Miss Moon asked.

"I said it!" shouted Mouse.
"And I am HIDING because I am SHY."

"But WHO, and WHERE are you?"
asked Miss Moon.

"I am Mouse, and I am
HIDING behind the CURTAINS!"

Miss Moon smiled. "Well dear," she said,
"now that we know
WHO you are
and
WHERE you are . . .

. . . why don't you come out
so that everyone can see you?"

Now, Mouse's mother had said to Mouse,
"Be sure to be good," so Mouse sighed,
and crept out from behind the curtain.

"That was a brilliant
hiding trick," said Bat.

"When I hide,"
said Owl,
"bits of me stick out."

"Me too," said Cat,
"and I have to remember
not to purr."

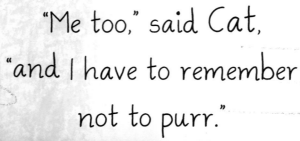

"I LIKE hiding,"
said Mouse.

"I know what,"
said Miss Moon . . .

" . . . let's play hide-and-seek
right now.
We've just got time
before midnight snacks."

Miss Moon closed
her eyes.

"1 2 3 4 5 6 7 8 9 10"

"Coming!" she cried. "Ready or not!"

Miss Moon found Owl easily.

Quite a LOT of him was sticking out.

SHADES OF NIGHT

THINGS THAT GO BUMP

WHY?

Miss Moon found Cat easily.

Cat was so pleased with her hiding place, she was purring rather loudly.

PURR PURR PURR PURR PURR

Miss Moon found Bat easily.

He had forgotten that
the fish tank was made
of glass and easy
to see through!

But Miss Moon
could not find
Mouse ANYWHERE.

"Mouse really is good at hiding," said Miss Moon.

"Let's all look for her."

So they looked inside
the paint pots . . .

. . . and they looked on the tops of cupboards
and they looked under a pile of special leaves.
But they couldn't find Mouse ANYWHERE.

"Oh dear," said Miss Moon.
"Mouse's mother WILL be cross
if we have lost her."

SPECIAL LEAVES

Then Miss Moon
heard a tiny laugh.
"That sounds JUST like
Mouse," she said.

"Tee hee," Mouse laughed again.
"You didn't find ME!"

"That's true, dear," said Miss Moon,
"but now it's time for midnight snacks,
so do come out, and we can all
have something nice to eat."

Mouse crept out from her hiding place.
She had been hiding in Miss Moon's
hat-flowers all along!

"Well done, Mouse,"
said Miss Moon happily.
"You are the best
at hiding!"

And Owl and Bat
and Cat
all agreed.

Mouse
was SO pleased,
she forgot all
about being shy.

And she NEVER
hid from
her friends
again . . .

. . . unless, of course,
they were playing hide-and-seek.